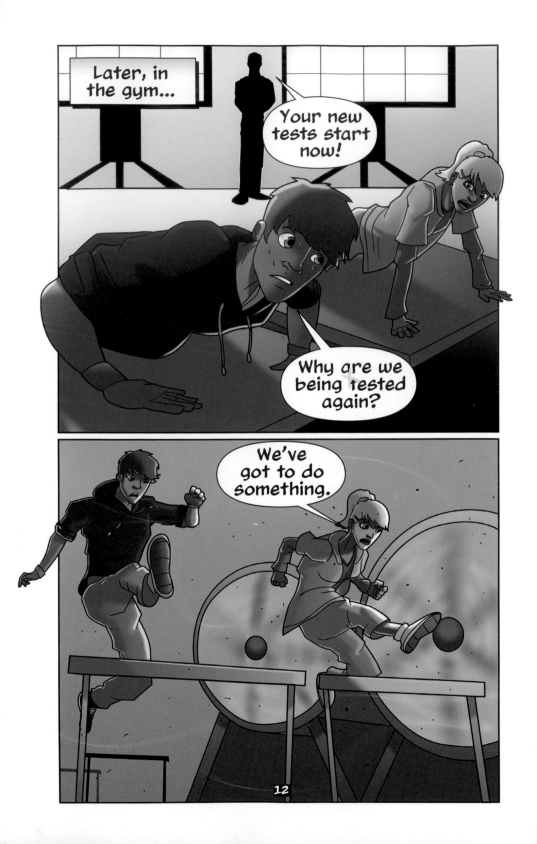

13

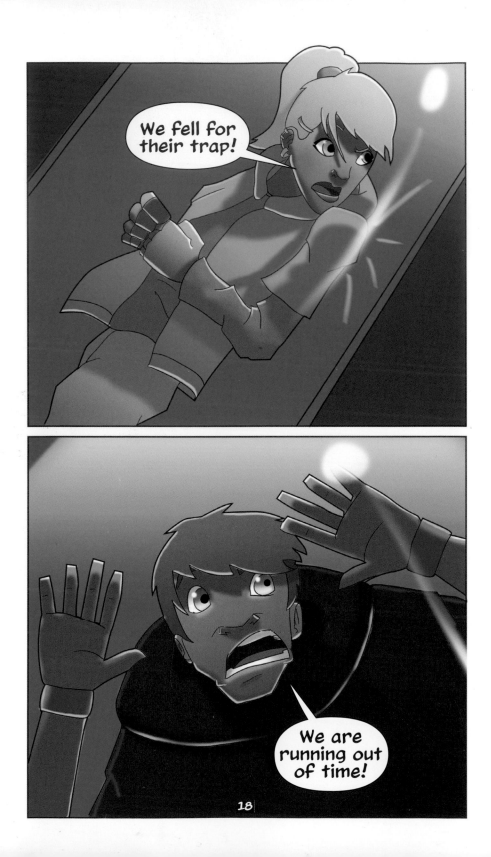

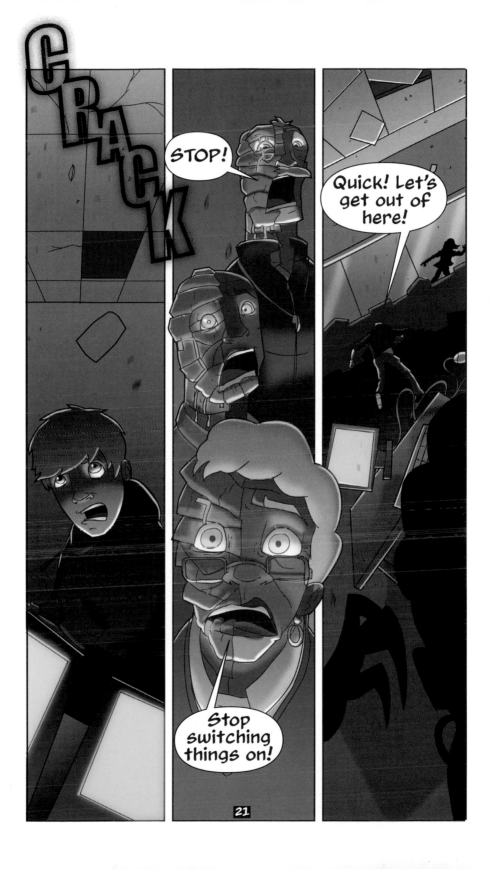

About SLIPSTREAM

Slipstream is a series of expertly levelled books designed for pupils who are struggling with reading. Its unique three-strand approach through fiction, graphic fiction and non-fiction gives pupils a rich reading experience that will accelerate their progress and close the reading gap.

At the heart of every Slipstream graphic fiction book is a great story. Easily accessible words and phrases ensure that pupils both decode and comprehend, and the high interest stories really engage older struggling readers.

Whether you're using Slipstream Level 2 for Guided Reading or as an independent read, here are some suggestions:

1. Make each reading session successful. Talk about the text or pictures before the pupil starts reading. Introduce any unfamiliar vocabulary.

2. Encourage the pupil to talk about the book using a range of open questions. For example, how would they feel if their school started testing them every day? What sports would they be best at?

3. Discuss the differences between reading fiction, graphic fiction and non-fiction. Which do they prefer?

For guidance, SLIPSTREAM Level 2 – Alien Academy has been approximately measured to:

National Curriculum Level: 2b
Reading Age: 7.6–8.0
Book Band: Purple

ATOS: 2.2*
Guided Reading Level: I
Lexile® Measure (confirmed): 250L

*Please check actual Accelerated Reader™ book level and quiz availability at www.arbookfind.co.uk